E
DI
Dickson, Anna H.

"Where's my
blankie?"

"Where's My Blankie?"

A SESAME STREET / GOLDEN PRESS BOOK

Published by Western Publishing Company, Inc. in conjunction with Children's Television Workshop.

FGHIJ

"Where's My Blankie?"

SESAME STREET
CTW
A GROWING-UP BOOK™

By Anna H. Dickson / Illustrated by Carol Nicklaus

Featuring JIM HENSON'S SESAME STREET MUPPETS

Malcolm Monster never went anywhere without his blanket.

He took it to breakfast.

He took it to the park.

He took it to play group.

He took it to the P & Q Supermarket.

Malcolm always took his blanket to bed, but not to keep him warm. To snuggle.

The day of Prairie Dawn's birthday party, Malcolm helped his mommy wrap the present and then he was ready to go.

"You won't need your blanket at the birthday party, dear," she said, putting the present in a shopping bag.

But Malcolm took it anyway.

Malcolm Monster never played anything without his blanket.

He played camping out.

He played Supermonster.

Malcolm used his blanket for everything.
He used it as a beach towel.

He used it as a Halloween costume.

When Malcolm's blanket got monstrously dirty, his mommy washed it.

And when it got ripped and torn and tattered, she mended it.
Malcolm didn't mind.

When fall came, the Monster family prepared to visit
Grandma and Grandpa. Mommy and Daddy thought
Malcolm should leave his blanket at home.

"You're too old to take it," Daddy said.

"It's too shabby," Mommy said.

"You don't mind leaving it at home this time, do you,
Malcolm?" they said.

But Malcolm did mind.

On the way to Grandma and Grandpa's house they stopped at Hasty Johnson's for lunch. Malcolm put his blanket in his lap as usual.

"Look, Daddy!" said Malcolm's sister. "Malcolm brought his blanket.

"Baby monster, baby monster!" she chanted.

"That will be enough, Monya," said Daddy.

While they ate lunch Mommy Monster again told the story of the blanket. Grandma Monster had made the quilt as a baby gift when Malcolm was born. When he was a tiny monster he had slept with it every night and had played on it every day.

"You see," she said, "Malcolm has always had his blanket."

She turned to him and smiled. "But Malcolm, you are getting to be a big monster. It's up to you, but I don't think that you need your blanket any more."

Malcolm thought that he did.

The Grandmonsters were joyful when the family arrived!

"I have a surprise for you," Grandma Monster said to Malcolm and Monya. "I made new quilts—one for each of you—out of clothes that you've outgrown!"

"Oh, thank you!" they said, giving her a monster hug.

That night, when Grandma peeked in at the sleeping youngster monsters, she saw that Malcolm was still sleeping with his blanket.

On the last day of the visit Grandma and Grandpa Monster and all the aunt and uncle and cousin monsters had a wonderful monster picnic. Malcolm played with his cousins right up until the minute he got in the car to go home.

There were many monster hugs and kisses and then the Monster family drove away.

"Good-by!" called the monster cousins. "Come back soon!"

Malcolm was so tired that he slept all the way home. Daddy carried him inside and tucked him into his own bed.

The next morning Malcolm had drunk his orange juice and was halfway through his Monsterberry Crunch when suddenly he stopped eating and put down his spoon.

"Where's my blankie?" he asked.

"Isn't it in your room?" asked Mommy. "Go look under your bed."

Malcolm did.

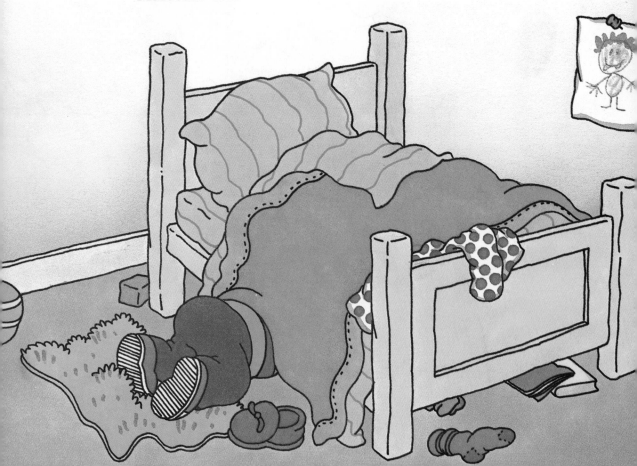

"It's not in my room!" he wailed. His stomach felt sick.

"Didn't you pack it in your toy bag?" asked Monya. "Go look!"

Malcolm looked in the toy bag he had taken to Grandma's. "It isn't here!"

"Maybe we left it in the car," said Daddy. "I'll go and see." But it wasn't there either.

"My blankie is lost! Where's my blankie?" Malcolm began to cry.

"Don't worry, dear," said Mommy. "We must have left it at Grandma's."

So Mommy called Grandma Monster on the telephone and told her about the lost blanket. Grandma looked in the kitchen, and outside under the apple tree.

Then she looked under the sofa—and that's where she found Malcolm's blanket.

"I'll mail it to Malcolm right away," she promised.

That morning Betty Lou came over and played
hopscotch with Malcolm.

Malcolm was very brave. He waited patiently for the
mail truck. But the only package delivered on the block
was a box of paperback books for Hooper's Store.

That afternoon Malcolm played
on the tire swing with Ernie and
Bert and the Sesame Street gang.

After dinner Malcolm listened to Mommy read a
story. When she finished, he asked, "How am I going to
go to sleep without my blankie?"
"You slept pretty well last night," said Daddy. "I'll bet
you can do it again."
And he did.

The next day Bert and Malcolm
set up an apple juice stand
on Sesame Street. Malcolm
was so busy that he forgot
to watch for the mail truck.

The next day Cookie Monster and Malcolm made
four dozen monster munchies.

"Malcolm," Mommy said, "a package just arrived for
you from Grandma. It must be your blanket."

"Oh, thanks, Mom," he said. "I'll open it later."

And Malcolm and Cookie Monster put the munchies
in the oven to bake.

Malcolm wasn't very hungry at dinner time. He told Mommy and Daddy and Monya all about his day. He was so tired that he was ready for bed right after dinner.

"I put your blanket on your bed," Mommy told him when he kissed her good night.

Malcolm yawned. "Thanks, Mom," he said. "I forgot all about it.

"Good night, everybody."